The Magic Pen

Written by Hiawyn Oram
Illustrated by Nick Schon

 Collins

Once there was a big man called Mr Big. His house was big, his car was big and his cat was big.

2

One day he tried to write a letter and he broke ten pens.
"I need a big pen," said Mr Big.

Mr Big went to the shops
to get a big pen.

But the man in the shop
forgot the ink.
"I'll make my own ink,"
said Mr Big.

He mixed and he mixed and he mixed.
Then he put in lots of water.

Mr Big filled up the big pen with his ink and said, "What shall we write?"
His cat said, "Write **Mouse**."

So Mr Big wrote **Mouse**.

At once a mouse ran over the paper.
Mr Big cried, "Wow!
This pen must be magic."

"Yes," said the magic mouse.
"You wrote **Mouse**, so here I am!"

"Quick!" cried Mr Big.
"What shall I write next?"

12

"**Fish**!" cried Mr Big's cat.
"**Cheese**!" cried the magic mouse.

13

"No, no," said Mr Big.
"We mustn't waste the ink!
Now, let me think …"

Then, with a shy smile on his big face, Mr Big wrote ... **Mrs Big**.

At once the doorbell rang.

There stood a woman
who was as big as Mr Big.

They were married three weeks and four days later.

The magic mouse and the big cat
went to the wedding.

Mr and Mrs Big, the cat and the mouse
all lived happily ever after ...

... with a little help from
the magic pen and ink.

slide

Mr Big's Magic Pen and Ink

23

Ideas for guided reading

Learning objectives: to relate story setting and incidents to own experience; to solve new words; to use various cues to predict and check meanings of words and help reading; to learn new words from reading; to interpret a text by reading aloud with some variety in pace and emphasis

Curriculum links: Numeracy: Shape, space and measure

High frequency words: there, was, big, house, he, ten, make, then, here, they, were, what, now, lived, after, but, man, so, with

Interest words: vinegar, sugar, orange juice, tea, cress, jelly, forgot, mouse, cheese, married

Word count: 247

Getting started

- Look at the front cover together and ask the children to predict what the story is about. How can a pen be magic?

- Walk through the book and discuss what is happening in the pictures. What can they say about Mr Big, and what happens when he buys a pen? How do the mouse and Mrs Big come into the story? Write the names of the characters on a whiteboard. Leave pp22–23 to look at later.

- Ask the children to practise a big voice for Mr Big and a small voice for the other characters.

Reading and responding

- Ask the children to read the story quietly and independently from the beginning. Remind them to use phonic cues and to check the detail in the pictures when they come to a difficult word, e.g. *sugar, vinegar, married*. During reading, prompt and praise each child where appropriate.

- Prompt the children to read the direct speech in role (for Mr Big and the mouse) with appropriate expression.